This Little Tiger book belongs to:

_____

_____

_____

For Joshua David Constant
and Hannah Linda Constant,
with love ~ *LC*

For Noah ~ *JC*

LITTLE TIGER PRESS
An imprint of Magi Publications
1 The Coda Centre, 189 Munster Road, London SW6 6AW
www.littletigerpress.com

First published in Great Britain 2000
This edition published 2005

Printed in China

2 4 6 8 10 9 7 5 3

Two Hungry Bears

Linda Cornwell and Jane Chapman

LITTLE TIGER PRESS
London

Big Brown Bear and
Little Bear shared a
cosy cave. They shared
each other's company . . .

and they shared
each other's food.
Little Bear nibbled
round the edges . . .

and Big Brown Bear
munched up the middles.
In this way, they got
along very well.

But one very bright
autumn day, Little
Bear woke up feeling
EXTRA hungry
and Big Brown Bear
woke up feeling
MONSTROUSLY
hungry!
"I'll buy some food
for both of us," said
Little Bear.
"That's very kind
of you, Little Bear,"
answered Big Brown
Bear sleepily, and
he crept right
back to bed.

Little Bear went out
shopping and bought
some things to take
back to Big Brown
Bear. But she found
she was so hungry . . .

that she ate everything
straight away –
pies and pastries,
peanuts and puddings,

chocolates and cheeses,
crisps and cakes –

from sides to middles,
middles to sides
AND BACK AGAIN!

Meanwhile, Big Brown Bear's tummy was
RRRRUMMMBLING rather loudly – so loudly
that the walls of the cave began to shake.
"I've been thinking," said Big Brown Bear,
"perhaps *I* should be out shopping for Little Bear."
So off he went with his big bag . . .

but when he had filled
it right up, he was so
hungry that he found
he could not wait.

He began by
munching just
the middles.

But then he set to work on sausages,
strawberries and sandwiches,
not to mention tangerines,
toffee apples and treacle tarts . . .

AND
hamburgers,
custard and
chips . . .

AND
biscuits,
spaghetti
and soup . . .

AND
pizzas, salads and
ice-creams . . .

AND
tomatoes,
jellies and
corn on the cob –
and one small
grape.

Big Brown Bear ate tops, bottoms,
sides and middles.
There was just no stopping him!

But when he had finished eating,
he began to feel very, very full
and very, very guilty.
He had left nothing for Little Bear.

Big Brown Bear staggered back home where
Little Bear was waiting patiently for him.
"Did you find any nice middles to munch?"
Little Bear asked him.
"*I can see that you did!*" she thought to herself.
Big Brown Bear could only nod his head.

"Did you come across any tasty edges to nibble?"
asked Big Brown Bear.
"*It certainly looks as though you might have!*"
he thought to himself.

They sat
down together –
rather carefully.
"I saved you half
of a cream cracker,"
said Big Brown Bear.
"It still has four
edges to nibble."
"I saved you three
quarters of a banana,"
said Little Bear.
"It's all middle –
no edges
at all!"

After a while, Big
Brown Bear yawned.
"I think I'll skip supper,"
he said. "I'm feeling
a little too tired."
"An early night will
do us both good,"
agreed Little Bear.
They spent an awfully
long time brushing
their teeth . . .

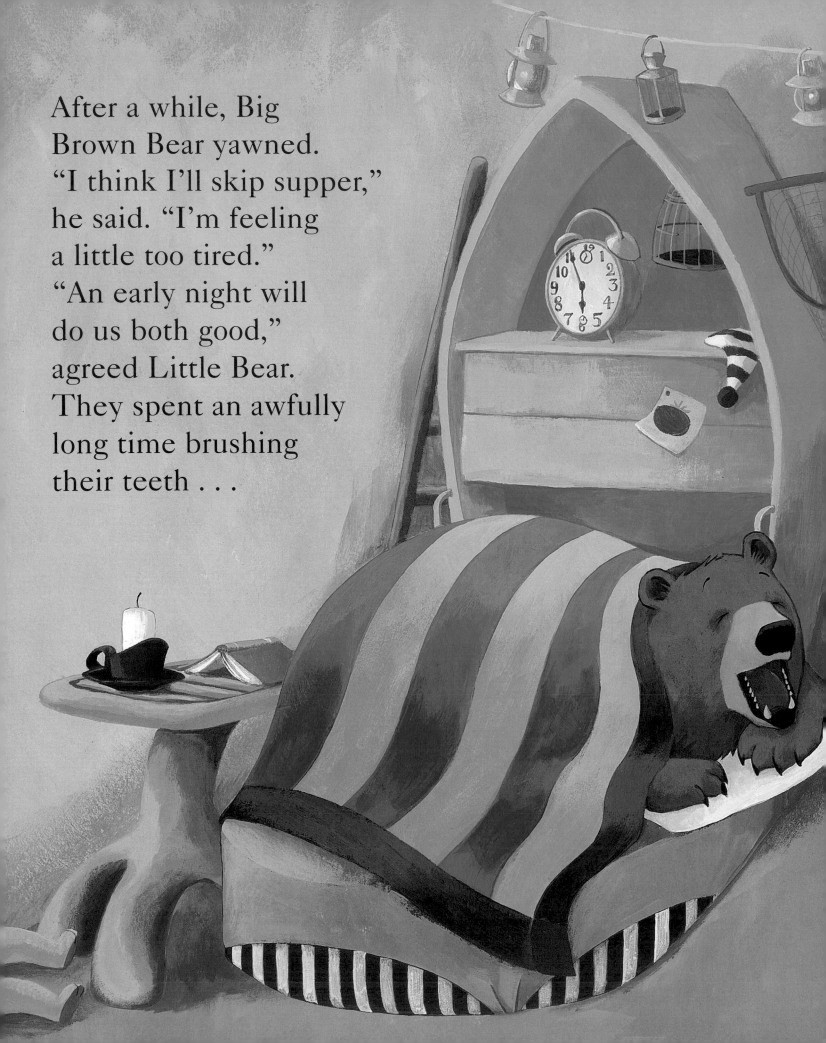

before Big Brown Bear snuggled into his
bed, and Little Bear crept quietly into hers.
"Let's collect the food together tomorrow,"
yawned Big Brown Bear.
But tomorrow was a long, long time away
because . . .

Big Brown Bear and
Little Bear slept, with
their tummies nicely full,
all through the winter until
SPRING!

Fantastic reads from Little Tiger Press

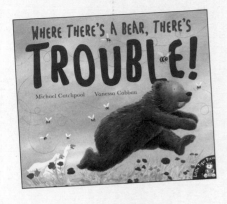

WHERE THERE'S A BEAR, THERE'S **TROUBLE!**
Michael Catchpool · Vanessa Cabban

You're Too Small!
Shen Roddie
Steve Lavis

BAA! MOO! WHAT WILL WE DO?
R.H. Benjamin
Jane Chapman

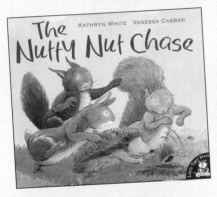

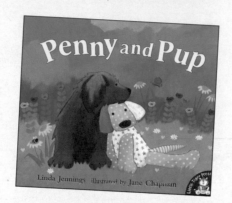

KATHRYN WHITE · VANESSA CABBAN
The **Nutty Nut Chase**

Penny and **Pup**
Linda Jennings illustrated by Jane Chapman

I don't want to go to bed!
Julie Sykes · Tim Warnes

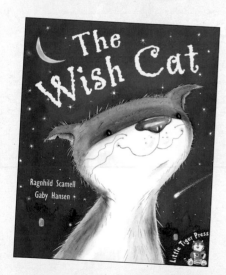

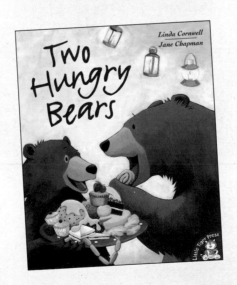

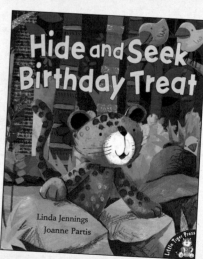

The **Wish Cat**
Ragnhild Scamell
Gaby Hansen

Linda Cornwell
Jane Chapman
Two Hungry Bears

Hide and Seek **Birthday Treat**
Linda Jennings
Joanne Partis

THE GREAT GOAT CHASE
Tony Bonning · Sally Hobson

For information regarding any of the above titles
or for our catalogue, please contact us:
Little Tiger Press, 1 The Coda Centre,
189 Munster Road, London SW6 6AW, UK
Tel: +44 (0)20 7385 6333 Fax: +44 (0)20 7385 7333
E-mail: info@littletiger.co.uk
www.littletigerpress.com